W9-CLS-557

EPIC

EPIC

SARINA BOWEN

ELLE KENNEDY

Copyright 2019 and 2020 by Sarina Bowen & Elle Kennedy. All rights reserved. Please respect the hard work of these authors.

Cover Photograph by Jane Ashley Converse. Cover Model Austin Loews.

Editing by Aquila Editing.

MY WEAKNESS IS HIM

Er ist meine Schwäche.
(German)

Minha fraqueza *é ele.*
(Portuguese)

Min svaghed er *ham.*
(Danish)

Mon point faible, je le connais. C'est lui.
(French)

Ö az én gyengém.
(Hungarian)

Il mio punto debole è *lui.*
(Italian)

Moje slabina je *on*.
(Czech)

CONTENTS

1. Wes   1

2. Jamie   9

3. Wes   17

4. Jamie   25

5. Wes   33

6. Wes   39

7. Jamie   47

A Love Letter from Wes to Jamie on Valentine's Day   57

Wesmie around the World   59

Also By Sarina Bowen & Elle Kennedy   69

1

WES

"You can't just decide to *be* Canadian," Blake Riley says, his beer glass clutched in one of his giant paws.

"Sure you can," Jess argues, lining up the cue ball for a tricky combination shot. "That's what I like about Canada."

"Nuh-uh. Canadian is a state of mind. I've got the Canada brain. You don't."

"Oh, you've got something, all right," she mutters under her breath.

"It's okay to be jealous, baby."

"I'm not jealous."

"Yeah you are."

"Oh my God, I'm not."

"Lying isn't sexy."

"*You're* not sexy."

"Don't be crazy now."

Jess gapes at him over her cue. "*I'm* the crazy one?"

I watch the entire exchange in amused silence. Blake and Jess love to argue with each other almost as much as they love each other. I glance at Jamie to see if he also finds the two of them ridiculous. But he's staring into his beer glass, lost in thought.

He's been awfully distracted tonight. And I have no idea why.

Jess finally shoots, and I can tell that she's not going to pull it off. Or rather—she wasn't. But at the last second Blake casually reaches down and nudges the ball toward the corner. And it drops into the pocket.

"Hey!" I argue. "Whose side are you on?" Blake and I are supposed to be partners against the Cannings. And we're winning.

"Shut up, ya hoser," Blake yawps. Then he gives me a big grin. "See? It sounds perfectly natural on me. Canadian brain."

"Did you really just throw the game for me?" Jess squeaks. She sets down the pool cue and leaps into his arms.

"Yeah, babycakes. Anything for you." Blake's beer sloshes violently against the side of his glass as he kisses her. "Is it time to go home? I'm planning an invasion of California with my Canadian missile."

"Jesus. TMI." I shudder as they continue to make out right in front of me. "We've been over this. I'm easily scarred. I thought Canadians were polite. Jamie, make them stop."

"Hmm?" My husband looks up suddenly. "Problem?"

I take a good look at him. Not that I mind the view. His

hair looks golden in the warm lighting of the bar, and his brown eyes blink back at me. But he's weirdly distracted. "You okay? You're kind of checked out tonight."

"Sorry," he says quickly. "Who won, anyway?"

"They did, apparently." I jerk a thumb toward Blake and Jess, who are staring into each other's eyes and exchanging kisses. "Maybe it's time to hit the road? You have an early practice, right?"

"Totally." He sets down his unfinished beer. "You brought the Jeep? I don't mind driving if you need me to."

"Yeah, I drove. But I got it. Should we pry them apart or just yell goodnight from a safe distance?"

Jamie finally glances at his sister and Blake. He scowls. "Keep it PG, kids. We're heading out."

"Don't wait up, Wesmie!" Blake says with a grin.

"Night!" Jess chirps.

Before we even turn around, they're back in each other's arms. "Do you think they're always like that?" I ask. "Or do they just lay it on thick to annoy us? You're the one with all the siblings. Tell me how this works."

"Uh huh," is all Jamie says. Then he pushes open the door to the bar, and a gust of chilly March air makes us both shiver.

THIRTY MINUTES later I come out of the bathroom to find Jamie already in our bed, arms tucked behind his head, expression thoughtful.

I shut off the light and climb in beside him, ready to

finally hear what's on his mind. Maybe it was something I said?

Or maybe not, because Jamie rolls toward me immediately, hand on my belly, fingertips sweeping across the skin above the waistband of my flannel pants.

I open my mouth to ask what's on his mind, but it doesn't quite work. Because his lips land on mine, and then we're kissing. I'm not an idiot. When the love of your life wants a make-out sesh, you don't toss that aside.

So I move closer, running a hand up his bare back, threading a flannel-covered knee between his bare ones.

Wait. Jamie isn't mad at me. Jamie is naked. I do a mental backflip at this realization, and kiss him a little more deeply. I miss him so much when I'm away. There's another road trip coming up, too. I'll be on the West Coast for days and days.

Jamie knows this. Jamie is a smart man. Very very smart. I groan, sliding my tongue against his. And then I turn my head in order to explore his jaw, testing the softness of his whiskers with my lips.

It's been almost three years since our first kiss. My life changed that rainy night in Lake Placid when Jamie pushed me up against the side of a roadside bar and kissed me. It was like falling into a fantasy from which I've never had to wake up. I suck on his neck, right under the line of his whiskers. He smells of minty toothpaste and the shower products we both share.

The room shifts, and I find myself on my back. My golden boy has escalated the situation by climbing on top of me and sifting his fingers through my short hair. His next kiss is hard, maybe even a little desperate.

"Jamie," I say against his mouth.

"Mmm?" He runs a hand across my chest and then pinches my nipple.

"You okay?" I'm loving the attention, but I can't shake the feeling that something is bothering him. When he's troubled, my guy won't always say what's on his mind.

"Really?" he rasps, kissing me again. "You want to chat right now?"

"With you? Always." I brace my hands on his shoulders, lock a heel against the bed, and then roll quickly. I've turned the tables, so now I'm looking down into his handsome, startled face. "Now spill, babe. You can't have this hot body until you tell me why you were so quiet tonight. I mean—you didn't even react when Blake claimed that sloppy Joe sandwiches were named after his uncle."

Jamie snorts. "That wouldn't even surprise me if it were true."

"Yet you didn't hear it. And I want to know why."

He turns his head to the side and sighs. "I had a weird day, is all. But it's nothing a couple of blow jobs can't fix."

"Weird how?" I press. "Tell me, and then we'll have more time for funzies."

He smiles, then runs a hand down my chest. "It's not that big a deal, okay? We had some scouts at the rink today."

"From where?"

"Ottawa." Jamie yawns before continuing. "The goalie scout. Again."

"They must be seriously interested in your man Chambers." Jamie is the goalie coach for one of the best teams in the Ontario Hockey League. He'll probably be named Head Coach for a major juniors team of his own in a few years. He's had three rock-star seasons just like I have. "This is exciting, right? They're going to draft your guy?"

Slowly, Jamie shakes his head. "That's what I thought, too. But then the scout pulled me aside and blew my mind. He said they had some pressing issues on their keeper bench. And would I consider coming to Ottawa on a two way contract for their farm team."

"Oh," I say quietly. "As a *player*. That's..." I break off, because I have no idea what to say.

It shouldn't be all that shocking, because Jamie was a prospect for Detroit right after college. He was a terrific goalie. *Is* a terrific goalie. But he made the unusual decision to forgo that life in order to coach young hockey players.

And to be in Ontario. With me.

"You gonna talk to them about it? You should," I add quickly, just so he doesn't think I'd be upset about it.

"I'm really not sure. I mean, I'm probably *days* away from a promotion that I really want. And I didn't move to Detroit because I didn't want to sit around waiting for a chance to play."

"If they need you badly enough in Ottawa, maybe it wouldn't be like that, though."

Jamie covers his eyes with one of his hands. "Yeah. That occurred to me, too. I do not want to think about this right now." His hand flops to the side again, and he looks up at me. "I bet you'll think twice next time before you push me off your dick to have a bedtime conversation." The corner of his mouth quirks up in a smile. "Won't you?"

"Yeah, I suppose that's true." I lower myself onto his body again. "Would it be insensitive of me to ask where we were before I so rudely interrupted you?" I kiss him once. Twice.

Until he smiles against my mouth. "Not rude at all. But I believe we were..." He nudges me, and I let him roll me onto my back again. "Here," he says, settling his hips against mine. "Now shut up for a few minutes so I can do what I do best."

I zip my lips together, and I'm rewarded by a hot mouth kissing a path down my neck, and onto my chest. His tongue comes out to play as he works his way down my abs. I spread my legs and groan, ruffling his soft hair as his perfect mouth gets ever closer to my rapidly hardening cock.

As my pulse leaps, I sink into the moment, trying not to think about how much I already miss Jamie during the season.

Or how long a drive it is from here to Ottawa.

2

JAMIE

"Jamie, hey," my boss Bill says when I enter his office for our morning meeting. "Have a seat." Smiling, he gestures to the only empty chair in the room. The second visitor's chair is occupied by Bill's boss, who I didn't expect to find at this meeting.

My pulse speeds up at the sight of Ron Farham. Ron's one of the top guys at the Canadian Hockey League, the organization that governs the three leagues that make up Major Junior hockey in Canada. He's kind of a big deal, and my palms grow damp as I settle in the plush chair next to him.

Behind his mahogany desk, Bill Braddock offers me another smile. Reassuring. "Relax, Canning. This is just a yearly review, not an execution."

Just a yearly review? Nuh-uh. This is the meeting where I find out if I got the promotion I applied for.

Assistant Coach. The big AC. Sure, it doesn't sound like the most glamorous job title, but it's a step up from my current position of Associate Coach, and it's one step closer to my ultimate goal—Head Coach.

Don't get me wrong, I love working one-on-one with my team's goalie and defensemen. And I know my efforts definitely contributed to us winning the Memorial Cup tournament last year. The jury's still out on this year, but the boys have been kicking ass this season, so a return to the championship isn't out of reach.

But just because I was a goalie myself doesn't mean I don't have ideas about offensive strategies, or the ability to coach the hot young forwards that enter the league every year. I need a change. I need a broader set of responsibilities.

During our last road trip, Bill all but confirmed I was getting a promotion. It means moving to a different team whose home arena is about forty-five minutes north of Toronto, but I'm not worried about the commute from downtown. And yes, it also means no longer working with Bill, but as much as I like and respect the man, change is good.

Now, as I sit there in the presence of Bill *and* Ron, I wonder if maybe...maybe I'm getting an even better position? Why else would someone from the CHL be here?

"Let's get right down to business," Bill says without preamble. "Ron and I have been singing your praises all season. What you've done with Chambers is truly something."

Ron nods enthusiastically. "The way you turned that kid around? Very impressive."

"He turned himself around," I argue, although I can't deny that Dale Chambers was an absolute nightmare at the start of the season. Chip on his shoulder, not to mention a God complex. Kid earned his teammates' dislike from day one, and it took many, many team-building attempts to create some camaraderie between him and everyone else. If a team doesn't like or trust their goalie, it could tank an entire season.

But all it took was a few conversations with Chambers for me to realize he was crying out for help. His father abandoned the family when Dale was six, and the parade of male "role models" courtesy of his mother's awful taste in boyfriends created a hostile home environment that had Dale acting out in school and hockey practice. His sheer talent as a goaltender caught the attention of his youth league coaches, who encouraged him to keep playing.

"I just listened to him," I tell my bosses.

"You're good with them," Bill says seriously. "The boys. You have a real talent for nurturing these kids, Canning."

My cheeks heat up, and damned if my chest doesn't puff up with pride. I *am* good with kids. I know I am. And the praise being poured on to me feels great, not gonna deny that.

"You're an excellent role model," Ron agrees.

The balloon of pride grows bigger, filling up my entire chest.

"With that said..." Bill starts.

Here it is. I almost rub my palms in glee. Promotion time.

"I know you were hoping to land as the AC for the Barrie team, but that position was offered to Hannigan this morning."

Pop! goes the balloon in my chest. Replaced with a rush of cold air.

"Hannigan?" I echo stupidly. Percy Hannigan? But he's the most recent hire for Toronto. I pretty much *trained* the guy.

What the fuck.

"Um." I swallow, then force myself to maintain a neutral tone. "With all due respect, sir, but...do you think Hannigan is qualified? He only recently joined the staff."

"He already has an existing relationship with Coach Shay," Ron Farham reveals. "Percy played for him in high school."

What. The. Fuck.

"We decided they'd make a good team," Bill says gently, clearly catching the dumbfounded expression I was trying to mask. "And we believe your talents lie elsewhere."

I frown. "Okay. Am I being sent somewhere else then?"

He shakes his head. "Not yet. We'd like to keep you here in Toronto until we find the right position for you."

Excuses excuses excuses! When he was a kid, my brother Brady used to stomp his foot and shout a litany of "*Excuses!*" whenever our dad told him he couldn't go surfing that day for whatever (valid) reason. And now here I am, shouting my older brother's ancient tantrum mantra in my head, trying hard not to let the words inadvertently slip out of my mouth.

But I know they're just feeding me bullshit excuses. Uh-huh, I'm sure they're *really* hunting for some super-awesome "right position" for me. Meanwhile, Percy fucking Hannigan got the promotion I wanted, because he's buds with the Barrie head coach.

What in the actual fuck.

The two men keep talking. Keep trying to tell me what a great job I'm doing in Toronto. *I know I'm doing a good job*, I want to yell. *That's why I deserve a promotion!*

I'm not quite sure what I say during the rest of the meeting. Not much, though. But I'm not about to channel my brother and throw a tantrum. I need employment, after all.

But I am not happy. At all. Although I smile through gritted teeth and exchange handshakes with Bill and Ron, I'm seething inside. It takes *a lot* to piss me off. Anyone who knows me can tell you that I'm the most chill, easy-going guy you'll ever meet. I hardly ever lose my temper, and I can count all the times I've raised my voice on the fingers of one hand.

And yet I'm practically shouting when I call Wes while exiting the building. "You won't fucking believe this! Those fucking motherfuckers!"

Dead silence.

"Wes?" I exhale in a rush. "You there?"

"Yeah. Sorry, yeah, I'm here." There's another long pause. "I don't think I've ever heard you use that many expletives in one breath."

"Sorry." I shove my free hand through my hair. "I'm just furious, babe. I can't even believe what just went down."

"Tell me," he says urgently, and so I do. I tell him how everything I've worked so hard toward for *three years* was snatched out of my grasp because of an asshole named *Percy*, and how I get to keep my title of Associate Coach while my superiors travel to Make-Believe Land to find me a better job.

"I mean...maybe they're not bullshitting you? Maybe they'll offer you something else?" Wes says in a weak attempt to console me. "It sounds like they're really happy with your work, and have faith in you as a coach."

"If they had faith in me, they'd give me the job I applied for. The job I earned." I release an angry breath.

"I'm sorry, babe. I know this wasn't what you'd hoped for."

"You're fucking right about that. I'm so fucking *pissed*." I notice a woman pushing a stroller speed up as she over-hears my potty mouth. "Ah, sorry," I say lamely, but she keeps glaring at me until she's out of sight.

Hysterical laughter bubbles in my throat. "I just scared a woman and her baby," I inform Wes.

"All right. That's it. Go home and pack," he orders.

"Pack?"

"Yes. You're coming on this trip with me."

I furrow my brow. "To the West Coast?"

"Yup. You need some chill-out time. You can see your family, hang out with me and the guys, come to the game. A whole forty-eight hours without thinking about this job bullshit."

I don't know if that'll be possible, but I appreciate that he's trying to help. "I guess I could do that," I say slowly. "As long as I'm back by Saturday for our Niagara game."

"We fly back Friday," Wes assures me. "Now quit wasting time. If you're not at the airport in the next hour and a half, the jet will leave without you."

"Errrrannnghhhh. Arrrmmmmhhh."

"Babe? You okay down there?" I call down the crowded table.

"Ohhhhrrrgh," is Jamie's answer.

Depending on the context, the noises my husband are making might alarm me. But one look at his blissed-out face tells the whole story. We're at an Oaxacan restaurant in the center of San Jose, with several of my teammates. Since it's game day, everyone is eating lightly.

Everyone except Jamie. He's in pig heaven right now. Literally. He's eating homemade tortillas spread with pork cracklings and bean puree and fresh guacamole. A pile of calamari is waiting its turn in front of him.

And we've only gotten to the appetizers.

"There's no place like home," Jamie says through a mouthful. "There's no place like home."

"Don't forget to click your heels together," Matt Eriksson cracks.

"I don't have to," Jamie mumbles, taking a sip of beer. "I'm already here. There's nothing as good as California Mexican food. Nothing."

"I'll bet the people serving Mexican food *in Mexico* might take issue with that," Eriksson points out.

Jamie shakes his blond head. "It might be as good. But it can't be better. Seriously. I'm never eating Mexican in Toronto again. There's no point."

"Are you harshing on Canada?" Blake Riley gasps.

"Maybe a little," Jamie admits. "But come on. California is heaven. I went surfing with my dad at dawn. And now there's a party in my mouth."

"This really is the best guacamole I've had in my entire adult life," Lemming agrees, reaching for another chip.

I take a sip of the soda I ordered, because nobody drinks before a game. I'm feeling pretty good about myself tonight, and all because I cheered up my guy. Jamie is like a sturdy plant—happy under most conditions, but occasionally in need of some extra sunshine. A trip to California almost always does the trick.

Also blow jobs.

"Excuse me, miss?" Blake says, stopping a tall waitress in a short dress.

"Yes? Can I help you?"

"Possibly. But I have a question. The menu says 'chapulines' are sautéed grasshoppers. But what are they really?"

The waitress smirks. "Exactly what it says, big guy. Grasshoppers are crunchy and delicious. We flavor them with garlic and lime. Are you ready to try some?"

"Uh..." My teammate blinks.

Jamie raises his hand into the air. "I will. Even if he won't. Some of us aren't scared."

There's a rumble of laughter at the table. "So will I," Eriksson says, throwing down, too. "Blake might not be able to handle it, but I'm game."

"*Dude*," Blake threatens. "Don't give me that macho bullshit. You're afraid of *heights*."

"You're afraid of *sheep*," Eriksson fires back.

"But not deep fried sheep," someone else adds.

They glare at each other.

"So—one order of chapulines, coming up!" the waitress says. And when she walks away, she's laughing to herself.

I can't resist leaping into the fray. "A hundred bucks says Blake won't eat two grasshoppers."

"Are you eating them?" Blake demands.

"Sure, dude. Jamie and I will match you bug for bug. They come with dipping sauces. Just pretend you're eating a crunchy pecan."

"A pecan with six legs," Jamie adds cheerfully. Our eyes meet, and his are twinkling. I feel such a rush of love when I see his smile. I want to throat-punch his boss for shafting him on that promotion. I really do.

It's fun teasing Blake, and we do it on the regular. But Jamie knows that the real measure of a man isn't whether he can eat a fried grasshopper. The real measure of a man is whether he can be a good partner, a hard worker, and a role model all at the same time.

Jamie is all those things. Why can't Bill Braddock see that?

"A hundred bucks from me, too," Eriksson says, tossing some bills onto the table. "Who else is in?"

The betting escalates. And soon the server is back with a new platter of food. She plops it down in front of Blake. "*¡Buen provecho!*"

"Does that mean—*nice knowing you?*" Blake grumbles. "Who's going first?"

Jamie reaches over, plucks a fried brown grasshopper from the plate and shoves it into his mouth. "Mmm. Nice chili flavor." He grabs a second one, dips it in the sauce and pops that one in his mouth too. He chews, smiling.

"Let's go, Blake!" I prod. "There's seven hundred dollars on this table that says you won't eat two of them."

"Seven hundred dollars, and your manhood," Eriksson taunts, picking up a grasshopper and dipping it in sauce. "But no pressure." He eats his in one bite.

"Fine," Blake says with a scowl. "Just a second." He takes his phone out of his pocket and holds it up to frame his own face. "J-babe, if for some reason I don't make it back, I just wanted you to know that I love you. I know you'll raise Puddles to be a fine dog. Oh, and your birthday present is in the bottom drawer of the bedside table." He taps the screen and looks up at us with a serious expression. "Make sure she gets that video, fellas."

"Will do," I say with as much gravitas as the moment calls for. Which is none.

Blake reaches toward the plate as if it might bite him. But he grabs a grasshopper between his big fingers. No— two of them. He's going with the all-at-once strategy.

"Do it! Do it!" I chant. And then everyone else starts chanting, too.

Suddenly we're *that* table—the loud, obnoxious one that other diners despise. And we're not even drinking.

Blake closes his eyes and opens his mouth. The grasshoppers go in. He chews...

We all lose our minds.

He swallows. Then he grabs Jamie's beer out of his hand and chugs it.

Our table erupts with applause.

I have the best job in the whole damned world.

WE HAVE to be at the rink pretty early. But they let Jamie into the players' entrance with me so that he can pick up comp tickets for himself and his parents.

"What are you going to do until game time?" I ask him.

"Heading back to the hotel. Returning some calls." His eyes dip.

"What kind of calls?" I hear myself ask.

"That scout wants to talk to me again." He sighs. "He's here in San Jose."

"Really?" I freeze, my hand on the locker room door. "Is that a coincidence?"

He shrugs uncomfortably. "I'm not sure. He wanted to meet me tonight, but I told him I was spending some quality time with the family."

"You're blowing him off?" I laugh. "Harsh."

"My head is not in a great place to listen to him," Jamie admits. "I need a couple of days to sort out my shit."

"I bet." I put a hand onto his shoulder and squeeze. "Sure love having you here, babe. This has been fun."

His brown eyes grow warm. "It's the best. I got a video of Blake eating the grasshoppers. That's getting edited later. If you have any soundtrack suggestions, I'm listening." He rubs his belly. "I'm never eating again, either. But the pain I'm feeling now was totally worth it for that mole sauce."

"Take it easy." I lean forward and plant a quick kiss on his jaw. "See you after the game?"

"Knock 'em dead, babe." He gives me a quick hug, and then heads down the hallway, looking for the GM's assistant and her stash of tickets.

SPIRITS ARE high while we stretch and suit up. I need a goal tonight. The Cannings will be in the stands, and I like to impress my in-laws. The Canning clan is the best thing that ever happened to me. They love me whether I score or not.

Still. Let's get some points on the board. I'm in the mood to win.

I'm taping up my stick when Coach lets out a whistle. "Gather round, kids! Starting lineups are posted. There's two things we weren't expecting. San Jose put Murray on the first line. And they're playing Pitti in the net."

"Yeah?" I perk up. I'd rather be firing on their number-two goalie. "That's an interesting choice."

"Go get 'em," Coach says, slapping me on the shoulder. "Warm-ups start in two minutes."

I snap on my helmet and do a set of slow squats to keep my quads warm. Then I follow my teammates out onto the ice. The clock has sixteen minutes on it—regulation warm-up time. It never feels like enough. I take my first quick lap. I'm watching the opposing goalie, and visualizing my shot. I mentally snap one into the upper left-hand corner. And then I think through my approach on the right.

I'm in the zone, which means I'm not paying attention to anyone outside the plexi. You learn to tune out the sounds of the stadium.

So it takes me a minute to notice that the name they're calling over the sound system is familiar to me.

Very familiar.

"Jamie Canning, please identify yourself to a security staff member. Jamie Canning."

What the hell is up with that?

4

JAMIE

"**J**amie Canning, please identify yourself to a security staff member. Jamie Canning."

My head jerks to the side, like a dog tilting one ear when he's trying to understand human speak. "Was that my name?" I ask my folks.

The three of us have just settled in our seats—third row, right behind the Toronto bench. One of the many perks of being married to the team's top scorer. At home games, I sit in the Wives and Girlfriends box, but to be honest, I prefer watching live hockey right near the action.

My mom wrinkles her forehead. "I think it might have been."

"Once again, Jamie Canning, please identify yourself to a security staff member."

Concern tugs at my gut as I rise from the seat I just plopped into. "I hope it's not about Wes," I start. But no, he's on the ice warming up and looks just fine. Shit, maybe Blake...? Nope, he's skating too.

"I'll be right back," I tell my parents.

My stomach churns as I descend the steps toward one of the exits. I spot a security guard and quickly approach him. "Hey," I say awkwardly. "I'm Jamie Canning? They just said my name on the PA?"

"ID please."

I hand over my license.

He glances at it before passing it back. The man touches his earpiece and relays something in a voice so low I can't hear what he's saying. Then he drops his hand and gives a brisk nod. "Follow me."

Where? I want to blurt out. But the dude is already marching off without waiting to see if I'm following.

I hurry after him, and my stomach does another queasy flip. This time it's because I was a gluttonous pig and stuffed myself at dinner, so speedwalking isn't good for my current state. Too many grasshoppers swimming around in my belly.

To my utter confusion, the guard deposits me at a small office near the visitors' locker room. When I enter, I find myself looking at Bern Gerlach, the head coach of San Jose. Two other men are also present, but I don't recognize them.

"Mr. Canning," Gerlach says, extending a hand. "Bern Gerlach."

"Um, right. Nice to meet you, sir."

He introduces the men beside him as an assistant at the GM's office, and a rep from the league.

"I'm going to cut to the chase because the puck drops in ten minutes," he says in a no-nonsense tone. "Our goalie's out and we're starting his back-up. You're on the NHL list of emergency goalies—can you suit up for us tonight as Pitti's back-up?"

I stare at him. "I'm sorry, what?"

He repeats the request—and yup, it sounds as ludicrous the second time around. I *am* on the emergency back-up list for the league, but nobody actually ever gets *called*. Emergency goalies are mythical creatures. Every now and then you hear stories about an accountant who got called up to play one period for New York, or a plumber who suddenly found himself filling in for an injured LA goalie. But those are practically fables, rare situations that allow an everyday Joe to live out his professional athlete dreams.

"Canning?" the head coach prompts. "Can you suit up?"

I snap out of my amazement. "Yes," I find myself blurting, because who would ever say *no*? "But don't you have someone local who can fill in?" *Shut up, Jamie.* "Like someone from your farm team here?" *Seriously, dude, shut up. Don't give away this wonderful gift.*

The GM's assistant answers in a grim tone. "Our minor league team is on the way back from a game in Bakersfield. The team bus is currently sitting in deadlock traffic on 101. There was a huge pile-up about an hour ago."

"He won't make it here in time," the head coach says flatly. "You're our best option at the moment. Are you good to go?"

"I'm good to go, sir."

"Great." He nods toward the league rep. "Thompson

just needs your John Hancock on this waiver, and then I'll take you to the locker room."

I'm wearing the opponent's jersey. Fuck. Wes is going to kill me.

These are my thoughts as a trainer hustles me down the chute, past the security, and onto the home bench.

None of the San Jose players really glance my way as I sit on the end in the backup goalie's traditional spot. The league requires that teams dress two goalies for a game, but the chances of me actually playing are slim to none.

The arena is alive with excitement as the two teams get into position. Wes is on the first line, taking the faceoff. I'm dying to stand up and wave at him like a total idiot. Or anyone on Toronto, for that matter. This is like winning the lottery and not being able to share a single dime with the people you love. I want them to get as big of a kick out of this development as I'm getting.

But my husband and his teammates are laser-focused on the game, as they should be. Almost immediately after the faceoff, Pitti is under attack. Toronto takes advantage of the absence of San Jose's starting goalie.

Pitti is good, though. For eleven minutes, he stops every shot that careens toward him, at one point making a diving save that sends my heart lurching to my throat. I'm not even playing and yet the adrenaline in my blood is high. And the churning of my stomach is even worse now. Nerves and a hundred servings of Mexican food don't go well together.

But Pitti's luck runs out when Matt Eriksson unleashes a slapshot that flies into the net, top right corner. Toronto is leading us 1-0—and how cute is it that I'm now referring to it as "*us*." I'm not actually a San Jose player. I'm a bench-warmer who's not going to see a second of ice time because Pitti is killing it.

My job is to sit here, occasionally opening the bench door to accommodate a quick line change. There are backup goalies who spend ninety percent of their time sitting here, opening and shutting this door. And people wonder why I skipped the minors to become a coach.

It's hella fun for one night, though. And I've never had better seats for one of Wes's games.

When the first period comes to an end, I once again try to catch the attention of anyone from Toronto, but those bastards are all arrogantly skating off toward the tunnel without a backward look. With a lead of 3-1, they have a right to feel cocky.

I trudge back into the locker room with the San Jose game for the intermission. My clothes are still there, on the bench. Just to be an asshole, I dig out my phone, remove my borrowed helmet and snap a selfie in the teal jersey. I text it to Wes. He won't see it until after the game, but this is a moment that needs to be memorialized.

"Hey, pretty boy," a player taunts. "Maybe save the photo shoots for after the game?"

"Cut him some slack, bro," someone argues. "This is a

big deal for the dude."

"Sure is." I glance over gratefully at the player who'd sided with me.

"Where you from?" the player asks. He's a rookie D-man.

"Grew up in Marin County, but I live in Toronto now. I coach juniors hockey."

"Cool!" His face brightens. "Toronto, huh? Kinda funny that you got called in for this game."

"Um..." It's so much funnier than he even knows.

"Hey, no fucking way," a voice snaps. I look up into the snarling face of Nik Sokolav, San Jose's star forward. He must follow the sports gossip sites because he obviously recognizes me. "This guy can't be our backup! Coach! What the fuck?" He stands up, pointing at me. "He's sleeping with the fucking enemy! If he ends up having to go in, he'll hand the game to Ryan fucking Wesley."

Now everyone is staring. Awesome.

"Look," I chirp before Gerlach can answer. "Nothing makes me happier than kicking the hubby's ass. We used to have one-on-one competitions when we were kids and I won my fair share of them. I know how to stop the asshole."

There are some nervous chuckles in the room.

"Leave the man alone," Gerlach grunts. "Put the puck into the net tonight, Sokolav, and then it won't matter who's in the net."

And then? That fucker does.

He scores back-to-back goals during the second period, tying the game. From the bench, I don't miss the tight set of Wes's jaw as he flops onto the bench after his shift. He's pissed. He doesn't like losing. But Toronto turns it around at the end of the second, taking the lead again courtesy of a bullet from Blake Riley.

The buzzer sounds and once again I leave the ice with "my" team, unable to signal to a solitary Toronto player. I do shout out, "Yo, Wesley!" at my husband's retreating back, which gets me a deep scowl from Sokolav. Besides, my yell is drowned out by the thousands of other yells reverberating through the arena. I guess my short stint as a professional hockey player isn't destined to be witnessed, but the story'll be just as good when I tell it to Wes and the guys after the game.

The third period kicks off. Pitti once again is under attack, and once again holding his own against Toronto's powerful offense.

At least until the dive. It's not as beautiful and fluid as the dive he took in the first period. This time it's clunky and all wrong, and two Toronto forwards accidentally collide with him when he's down. There's a scuffle, and Pitti is blocked from my view. Whistles blow. The refs skate over to the net.

Relief washes over me when Pitti is helped up. He's okay. He made the save and took a couple of hits, but—

He's not okay, I realize.

He's cradling his stick arm, holding it tight to his chest. One of the refs is urgently speaking to him, and Pitti begins shaking his head. His padded shoulders droop slightly as he begins to skate away from the net.

On the bench, all eyes turn to me.

5

WES

Injuries suck. They really, really suck.

With that said, we're already beating San Jose by one, and now we're about to play the last fourteen minutes facing their *third-string* goalie? We'll be up by a dozen goals by the time this game ends.

I feel for Tim Pitti, I really do. He's clearly in pain as he heads for the tunnel toward the locker room. I wasn't on the ice for that play, but Blake said he heard a bone snap. The mere thought makes me shiver.

Injuries come with the gig, though. And while I sympathize with Pitti, I'm not complaining about this latest development.

"Who's the back-up's back-up?" Lemming asks blankly.

"No clue," Eriksson answers.

"It's that dude," Blake supplies, his gloved hand jerking toward the home team's bench.

I snort. "No shit, Sherlock. But what's his name? Have we faced him before?"

Our gazes are all glued to the San Jose player skating toward the net. His mask isn't on but his back is to us so we can't see his face. And his jersey doesn't have a name, just the number 33. At the net, he slaps his gloves on, then turns slightly, flashing a profile.

"Kinda looks like J-Bomb," Blake remarks.

"That kinda *is* J-Bomb," I growl, shooting to my feet. Well, my skates.

What the *hell* is happening? Why is Jamie wearing a San Jose uniform and manning their net?

I'm two seconds from vaulting over the wall when I get a sharp reprimand from Coach. Also, the PA system chooses that moment to announce that a one mister Jamie Canning is now the goaltender for San Jose.

Amazed laughter spills out of my mouth. He's on the emergency goalie list, I suddenly remember. He's filling in for an injured Pitti.

"He's giggling like a madman," Blake tells our teammates. "Wesley's lost it."

"Do you blame him?" Eriksson starts laughing too. "Canning's in net? Shit, this is epic."

"Epic," Blake echoes.

And then there's no more time for discussion, because a new faceoff begins and suddenly I'm watching my own teammates play against my own husband.

So. Fucking. Trippy.

It doesn't take long for the memories to flood my brain. Jamie's skill with the glove. His lightning-fast reflexes. The concentration, and the sheer calm—that's what always used to impress me about him when we faced off in college. He never, ever lost his cool. Nothing fazed him when he was tending that net.

"Change it up," Coach barks, and my line hops off the bench and takes the ice. I'm skating center, with Blake at my left and O'Connor to my right. Our D-men are Laurier and Matin. Our five best players, all zeroing in on Jamie Canning.

But he can handle it. He stops Blake's wrist shot, makes a save on the rebound, and then flicks the puck to a San Jose forward, who flies away with it. Now we're on defense. We spend the rest of our shift trying to stop San Jose from scoring on us. I'm out of breath by the time Coach calls for another line change. I heave myself over the wall as sweat drips down my face.

"Look at J-Bomb go!" Blake crows.

Like I can look at anything else. He's fucking *incredible*. He makes three more saves on this next shift, and then, to our dismay, one of the San Jose D-men capitalizes on an errant rebound and gets a lucky wrister past our goalie.

The game is tied. The hometown crowd is screaming, encouraging their guys. The few Toronto fans in the stands shout their own encouragement. Their energy fuels me as I take the ice again. Five minutes left—that's plenty of time.

I win the faceoff and dump the puck. Blake gives chase and gets his stick on it, snapping the puck back to me. But it's stolen by a D-man and San Jose is on the attack again. This time our goalie holds them off, and when the puck lands on my stick, I suddenly find myself on a breakaway.

Adrenaline sizzles through me as I charge the opposing net, where Canning stands guard.

This feels familiar. So fucking familiar. And I swear he sticks his tongue out at me when he denies me the goal. His glove closes around it, and frustration follows me all the way back to the bench.

It feels familiar because it *is* familiar. The one-on-one shootouts we had when we were kids are branded in my memory. Particularly because the last one led to my mouth on Jamie's dick. Our summers at hockey camp in Lake Placid were the best of my life. It's where I fell in love with Jamie. It's where we reconnected, and where he fell in love with *me*.

Jesus, how far we've come. Childhood friends, to lovers, to husband and husband.

Life is a beautiful thing.

When I play hockey, I'm always riding a high, but tonight it's two highs. It's adrenaline and excitement, and pure fucking love as I watch Jamie make four more saves over the next few minutes. When there are two minutes left, Eriksson takes a stupid penalty and San Jose gets themselves a juicy power play. I'm on the ice for the penalty kill, but the sharks are hungry, and thirty seconds in, they score.

The home crowd goes wild.

Toronto isn't able to tie it up. We lose to the home team, and while I'm disappointed, I also can't deny that I'm secretly happy for Jamie. His teammates swarm the ice and I lose sight of him in the massive show of celebration, but I know he must be over the fucking moon. And I'm glad for him. He deserves every bit of praise that's going to be poured on him tonight.

He deserves the world.

"**W**here. The fuck. Are we?" Blake asks, his eyes roaming the sleek, achingly hip room. "Silicon Valley does weird things to its bars."

He's not wrong. I'm holding a twenty-two-dollar cocktail, while blue light and techno music washes over us. "This is how I'd picture a bar on the Starship Enterprise."

"Nah," my teammate Will O'Connor says. "Where are the alien women with three tits?"

Forget the alien women. Where is Jamie? I take a sip of my over-priced cocktail and scan the room again. I'm aching to see his blond head pop out of the crowd. But no. It's just us.

After their win, San Jose sent a messenger to our locker room to tell us to meet 'em here. *You can have your goalie back after we buy him a drink*, the note said.

So I guess Jamie made some new friends tonight. He must be out of his mind right now. Honestly, my head is sort of blowing up with ideas about what might happen next. Was that Ottawa scout in the stands tonight when Jamie became San Jose's hero? I bet he was.

My man's whole life is about to change. And I feel *all the things*. Excitement. Astonishment. Disbelief. Worry. And—fine—a twinge of fear. He won't have as much time for me now. I don't need to be the center of attention. But I like being the center of *his* attention.

But I push that ugly emotion back into its cave. This is Jamie's night and I can't wait to watch what happens next.

Some of my teammates hit the dance floor, burning off their post-game energy. Lemming corners a leggy woman at the bar and starts turning on the charm. But I only slurp my drink and watch the door.

Just when I'm sure he's been kidnapped by my opponents, that golden head bobs into view, surrounded by a bunch of guys in teal jackets. I feel a rush of relief that doesn't make a whole lot of sense. And then I'm on the move, crossing the space, plopping my empty glass down on the nearest surface and hug-tackling him like I've needed to do all night.

"Hey!" he says with a laugh as I squeeze him. "Sorry about your scoreless period. Better luck next time."

The corners of his eyes crinkle with his smile, and everything is right in my world. "I'll get you next time." I take his handsome face in two hands and smack a kiss onto his cheek.

When I step back, a whole bunch of hockey players are staring at me. Pitti—the goalie whose arm is now in a sling—looks particularly stunned. As if *I'm* the alien with three tits.

They already know I'm *that* guy—the dude who's married to a dude. But apparently they've never seen it up close.

"So are we drinking or what?" Jamie says easily.

"Yeah," Nik Sokolav says, snapping out of it. "And Pitti is buying, because you saved his ass tonight."

"Aw, man," Pitti says with a chuckle. "Fine. Cheap beer for all my friends."

"Cheap beer here is nine bucks," someone points out. "Ouch."

"And don't forget your thirsty opponents," I put in. "We lent you Toronto's best goalie coach. It's time to pay up."

"We better get started, then." Pitti slaps Jamie on the back with his good hand and leads him toward the bar.

SEVERAL BEERS later I'm feeling high on life. Jamie is busy exchanging war stories with his new friends from California. But I'm making plans. It's a four-and-a-half-hour drive between Toronto and Ottawa. But a little research on my phone shows me a couple of towns between Toronto and Ottawa. Like Belleville and Kingston. We could buy a small house on Lake Ontario, and rent Jamie a studio in Ottawa.

On the nights when both teams are at home, we could make the two-hour drive and meet in the middle. It would be our getaway place. Also, if Jamie is in the minors for a while, his season would be shorter than mine by a couple of weeks.

And we'd have our summers. Sure, they're only six

weeks long. But I fell in love with Jamie over a few summers that weren't much longer than that, right? He's made all the sacrifices so far. I'm willing to make some for him.

When it's finally time to leave, I'm just bursting with ideas. They come spilling out in the cab on our way back to the team hotel.

"...And you'll be an even more valuable coach with some pro experience," I point out. "When you go back to coaching—and I know you'll want to—you'll have your pick of jobs."

Jamie listens patiently to all of this word vomit. It's hard to stop me when I get on a roll. We're all the way back to the hallway outside of our hotel room by the time I finally take a breath and unlock the door with my key card.

He walks in ahead of me, tossing his wallet on the desk and dropping a shopping bag the San Jose players gave him on our way out. There's a teal jersey in it that he wore tonight during his NHL debut.

Wordless, Jamie strips off his jacket and then his shirt. Then he flops backward onto the bed and stares, motionless, at the ceiling.

I might have blown his mind a little. I'll give him a minute before I launch us into victory lap sex. "I'm just gonna brush my teeth."

"No."

"No?" I pause in the doorway of the bathroom. "But I ate some weird bar snacks. I think they were gluten-free pretzels."

"No, I mean...I don't want to drive two hours every four days just to see your face."

"Oh." I swallow. "Okay. There's seventeen flights a day on Porter. That's my other idea. It's a one-hour flight time."

"Wes." Jamie sits up suddenly. "I had a great time tonight. Except when I thought I was going to barf."

"Were you nervous?" I ask, trying to understand.

"No! But I ate a lot of Mexican food. The first dive nearly broke me. But that's not the point." He shakes his gorgeous head. "I had a lot of fun, but it was just that. A wild night. And now I have more than five calls from that scout on my phone."

"He'd be crazy not to call you tonight," I point out. "He's probably peeing himself wondering if any other teams are after you."

Jamie makes an impatient noise. "Look, it *is* a fun story. My parents will be dining out on that for years. The sports blogs are going to eat it up. But I bet not one of them points out the unfair advantage I had tonight."

"What advantage?"

"I know you guys so well. I watch every Toronto game. I personally know every player on every line. Sure—I went in cold. But Blake's first wrister? It was like watching old video. I knew it was coming. That period was, like, optimized for my enjoyment. And it will never happen again."

"Well, sure, not exactly like that, but—"

He holds up a hand to silence me. "Here's the thing? I don't want my whole life to turn on a cute story, or a sound bite. If Bill Braddock called me right now and offered me the promotion I was supposed to have, I'd take it in a hot second."

Oh.

"I'm a good goalie, Wes. But I'm a *great* coach. I'm honestly kicking myself right now, because I should have pushed harder for that job. I should have made more noise. I blew it. That's been hard to accept. But I won't let a fun accident derail me from what I'm really supposed to be doing."

I sit down heavily on the bed beside him. I spent the evening galloping off in one direction, and it's not easy to rearrange my thinking. Again. "So you don't want to go to Ottawa at all?"

Slowly he shakes his head. "We'd never see each other. If you were in *prison* I'd be allowed more conjugal visits than we'd get if I move to Ottawa."

I bark out a laugh. "Let's not test that theory."

"Wes." Jamie beckons to me. And when I lean in, he wraps his arms around me. "I love you so hard. But don't plan this for me, okay? I know it's hard for you to understand, because you love your job so much. But I love mine, too."

"I know," I say quickly, wrapping my arms around his sturdy body. "I know you do. You were just so *amazing* tonight. I can't even handle it. I've never had more fun. Ever."

"Is that right?" Jamie thrusts a knee between my two legs and grabs my ass suggestively. "We have all kinds of fun, though. Half the time you can't even remember your own name afterwards."

"True." His skin smells like locker room soap, and I want more. Burrowing closer, I kiss his neck. "Fine. I won't try to plan your life. But does that mean I have to call off the goon squad I hired to teach Bill Braddock a lesson?"

"Yeah." He sighs. "Save the violence for the rink. This is a problem I have to solve by myself."

"You know I'd do anything for you. Even drive to Bellewood to do you."

Jamie snorts. "Belleville."

"Yeah. There, too."

He laughs and then kisses me.

JAMIE

When I step out onto the ice on Saturday morning, my head is full of plans for the Niagara game. We've got an hour for morning skate, followed by another hour for watching film. Then I'll have to let my guys take some time off for lunch, because the faceoff is at four.

But just as I skate my first few strides forward, every kid on the team lets out a shout and then rushes me. Four seconds later I'm swarmed by a pack of rowdy, laughing sixteen to twenty-one year olds. They actually hoist me into the air, all talking at once.

"Oh my God, that save on Wesley!"

"Fucking awesome!"

"Fire!"

"We were *dying*."

"Just here to entertain you," I chuckle, trying to get back onto my feet.

"Are you going to go pro?" my goalie wants to know. "That scout from Ottawa wants you more than me."

This again? "I'm not going anywhere." Not even to Barrie, apparently. It still stings that I didn't get that job. And out of the corner of my eye I can see Bill Braddock watching me from the top of the stands, where he's sitting with the assistant coach and a couple of other guys.

The pressure is on, then. We have to win this one.

I clap my hands together. "Okay, guys. Party's over. We're going to beat Niagara in a few hours, but only if we can shut down their offense. Let's do some D-drills before we watch film. Taylor—set up the cones for an odd man rush."

"Okay, Coach." He skates off.

Part of my job is to know which guys I can always count on to set the tone. Taylor is always open for business. "Trapatski! Stop wagging your jaw and set up for the rush. Let's move."

Bill and his crew stay in their seats, watching. It would be nice if the head coach or his assistant would get his butt down here and address his team, but I guess you can't have everything.

I'm feeling feisty today. I really am.

"Line up, guys! Move!"

EVERYONE IS sweaty by the time I'm done an hour later. Including me. "Hit the locker room!" I call after my whistle. "Video in thirty."

I'm the last one off the ice. And *now* Braddock is waiting at the bench? "Got a second?" he says.

Not really, I almost snap at him. I'm not a stupid man, so I hold it back. But I still feel frosty toward him. It's not a great way to feel toward your boss, but I guess I need a few more days to get over my disappointment.

"Sure," I mutter. "But we're watching video soon."

"I know. But I got a few things to discuss with you beforehand. First of all, I never had so much fun in my life as I did watching that San Jose game."

In spite of my grumpiness, a smile breaks out on my face. "It *was* fun."

"I know the Ottawa team is trying to lure you away from here to back up their back-up goalie. We're lucky you aren't that interested."

"You *are* lucky." It just pops out as I sit down on the bench to unlace my skates.

Bill only grins. "I know, kid. I know. And I can see on your face that you're not over the Barrie job. But that's not the right fit for you. You're overqualified to be that coach's assistant. And like Ron and I told you, we thought you deserved a different position."

My hands freeze on the laces. "Overqualified?" That makes no sense. Assistant Coach is the next job on the ladder. I lift my head quickly. "What the heck does that mean?"

"Jamie, I'm going to cover your video session, okay? There are some guys I want you to meet. They came up from Mississauga to get to know you better." He jerks his thumb toward the stands.

I squint at the coaches sitting in the distant seats. "Mississauga?"

He thumps me on the back. "Go talk to them."

I GET HOME AROUND SIX-THIRTY. When I push open our door, a shirtless Wes calls to me from the kitchen, where he's staring into the refrigerator. "How'd the game go, babe? And what do you want to do about dinner?"

"Dinner," I repeat slowly. My head is elsewhere.

"Yeah, dinner? That meal that you sometimes cook but we sometimes eat out?" He rubs his perfect abs. "I'm starved."

"I completely forgot what I wanted to do about dinner." I completely forgot everything I'd been thinking about until the guys from Mississauga blew my mind.

"You won your game, though?" Wes says, cocking his head to study me. "I saw the final score was four to three. Figured we could go out to celebrate."

"Celebrate." That word snaps me out of my haze. "Yes. Let's go out. No! Let's order in."

Wes tips his head back and laughs. "Which is it, babe?"

"Order something for both of us. Anything. I'm going to open a bottle of wine. There's something I want to discuss."

He shrugs. "Anything? Even Canadian Mexican?"

"Anything but that," I insist as I run by him toward our bedroom. "I'm going to change and open the wine. Meet me on the couch in five."

"Yes, Coach Canning. Hey—bring me a shirt?"

I'm so spacey that I forget the shirt. It's possible that my subconscious just wants to skip to the part of this evening where I'm removing his shirt again, anyway. We're going to have all kinds of celebrations, including the naked kind.

After I set two glasses of wine down on the coffee table, I fling myself onto the sofa beside Wes.

"Now spill," he says. "Did you talk to Bill?"

I open my mouth to answer, but Wes isn't done.

"—Did you tell him that you deserved that job? Did he read the story on the *Sports Illustrated* blog?"

"Wait, there's a story on *Sports Illustrated*?"

"'Family Feud' is the title they went with." Wes laughs. "There's a perfect shot of you stopping my shot. We gotta frame that sucker and hang it on the wall."

"Yeah. Awesome. Can I tell you my news now? I got transferred. And promoted."

"Really?" My husband's eyes widen. "To Barrie? Please don't say Ottawa."

"No! To Mississauga."

"Oh," he says carefully. "That's not too far from here, right?"

"Nope," I agree. "Only twenty-seven minutes down the Gardiner."

His eyes brighten. He dives across my lap, spreading out on the surface of the couch. "Shit. I got really worried when you said transferred."

I reach down and fluff his hair. "This is a good kind of transfer. I'll miss Bill, but it's all worth it. Don't you want to know what the job is?"

He rolls a little so he can look up at me. "Assistant Coach, right?"

I shake my head.

Wes's eyes practically bulge. "What, then?"

"Head Coach. I'll be the youngest Head Coach of a CHL team since...ever. Since the league was formed."

Wes sits up quickly. "You're *kidding* me! That's incredible!"

"I'm pretty pumped up. I mean—I'm a little stunned. They're announcing it next month, and then I'll be splitting time between Toronto and Mississauga until the end of the season, getting up to speed."

Wes is just staring at me now. "The youngest *ever*."

"That's what the man said." I think my jaw nearly fell off when the coach told me he was retiring and had handpicked me for the job.

"*Babe*." Wes scoots closer and takes my face in his hands. "You're a fucking rock star." Then he kisses me.

Ah. See? A shirtless Wes climbing into my lap is just the kind of celebration I'd been planning tonight. I pull him in with both hands.

He smiles into our kiss. "Maybe the pizzas I ordered will be a little late."

"Mmm," I agree, running my hands over his tatted biceps. "Pizza takes time." I tug on his leg until he straddles me properly.

"Congratulations on your win," he says between tongue-tangling kisses.

"What am I winning?" I tease, my hand coasting over his ass. "This?"

"Maybe," he grunts, kissing my neck. "If we have ti—"

The doorbell rings.

"WESMIE!" shouts Blake from right outside our door. "This fucking picture! I got a print and a frame! It's *epic*!" The sound of a giant fist pounding on our door is deafening.

We both groan.

"Stop makin' out on the couch and open this door!" There's another sound. A jingle. "Never mind, I got my key." The door bumps open a second later, and Blake's silly grin appears in the doorway. "Ooh, wine. Pour me a glass? Look at this!" Blake holds up a framed photo.

I get up and maneuver around the coffee table so that I can see it better. The photo shows me in full goalie gear, brow furrowed, getting my glove on Wes's shot. The WESLEY on the back of his jersey is just visible to the right.

Blake has somehow put a speech bubble over my head that says, "NOPE!"

I bust out laughing. Because it *is* epic. There is no better word.

"Did you guys order some food or something?" Blake asks. "It's time to put the chow in the mow. And Jessie's working the night shift."

Wes and I exchange a glance. I nod.

"How does pizza sound?" Wes says with a sigh.

"Awesome. I'll just get myself a wine glass."

"Thanks for being so good about all this," I tell Wes.

"About what? You getting your dream job? How else would I act other than fucking thrilled?"

"I mean, thanks for putting up with how moody I was over this job stress." I sit back down on the couch and put my feet in Wes's lap. "The Head Coach needs a foot rub."

"I thought I was the *head* coach in this relationship." He gives me a sleazy wink.

"You can show me later," I agree with a lewd grin.

"TMI!" Blake crows from behind the counter.

We both glance in his direction at the same time. And then back at each other. "Teach him a lesson?" Wes whispers.

"Yup," I agree.

And then we lunge for each other. Wes wraps his strong arms around me and dives into the kiss, sliding me onto the couch and then dropping his firm body over mine.

It's supposed to be a joke. But the second Wes's lips find mine, it's not all that funny anymore. I love this man, and I am so fucking lucky to have him in my life.

"Cheezus!" Blake yells. "No tongues! Aw, *dude*s. Well, I'm choosin' the TV channel. It's going to be something Canadian AF. Like the ice fishing championships."

Blake babbles on, but it's just background noise now. Eventually he joins us in the living room and we quit making out, but I can feel Wes's hungry gaze on me as I sip my wine, and I know we'll be all over each other again once our friend leaves. But for now, we let the anticipation build and content ourselves with the wine and the company and the joy of just being together.

Life is good.

No, it's *epic*.

The
End

A LOVE LETTER FROM WES TO JAMIE ON VALENTINE'S DAY

Babe–

I followed all the guys into a card shop in Boston last week, because somebody realized that Valentine's Day was around the corner, and none of 'em wanted to be in the doghouse.

So I started looking at cards just to pass the time. I'd never bought anybody a Valentine before. There were some surprisingly queer-friendly choices. There is this one that says on the cover, "I love your face." And when you open it: "Also, your butt."

Tell me that's not gay? C'mon.

So then I found this one with the snuggling cats on it. And, as you now know, the inscription is, "I want to spend all my lives with you." Insert the eyeroll, right?

Well. It was time to go, so I got in line with the other guys and bought this card as a lark. I thought I'd give it to you ironically, because Valentine's Day is for saps and men who need a piece of folded paper to make the wife happy.

Only here I am on Valentine's Day, writing this out before I leave for the morning skate. And you're still asleep in our bed, your face in the pillow. You look as snuggly as the cats on this card. And all I want to do is climb back into bed and hold you until you wake up and kiss me.

Yeah, okay. So it turns out this card isn't ironic at all. Guess I'm not the hipster I thought I was. I love you, and I <u>do</u> want to spend all my lives with you. If that makes me a sap, I guess I can't help it.

Happy Valentine's Day, Jamie. I'll be collecting my kisses later.

Love you,
Wes

WESMIE AROUND THE WORLD

Dear Reader,

When we set out to write Him, we just had no idea. We didn't know we were writing a book that would hit best-sellers lists. We didn't know Jamie and Wes would be translated into twelve other languages on four continents.

There are audio books, too! We are tickled to hear Wes say "my weakness is him" in Danish and Portuguese!

Here's a sampling of the international covers our publishers have lovingly given these books.

Thanks for all you do, readers!

Love,
Sarina & Elle

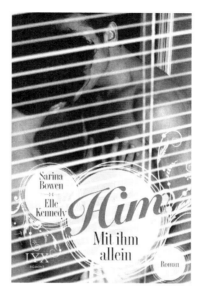

Lyx Verlag (German)

Lux Verlag (German)

Always (Italian)

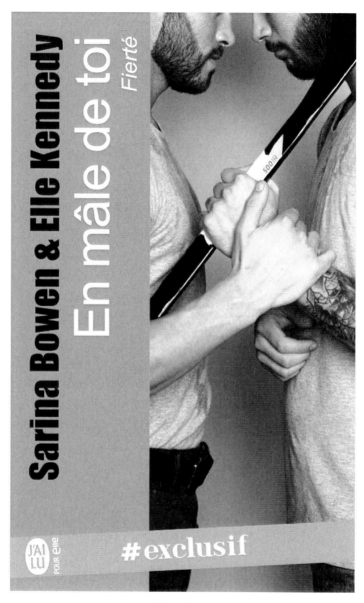

J'ai Lu (French)

J'ai Lu (French)

Flamingo (Denmark)

Flamingo (Denmark)

Companhia das Letras (Brazil)

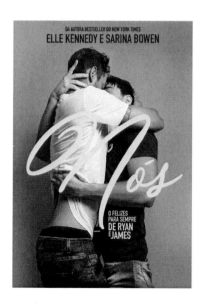

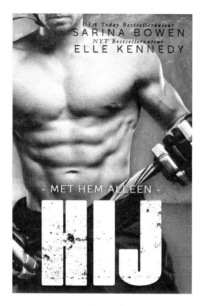

SVG (Dutch)

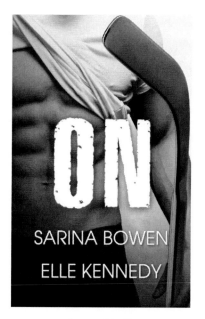

Baronet (Czech)

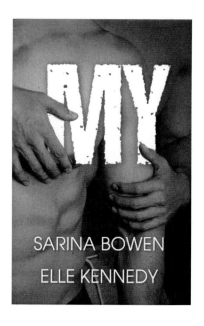

Kaewkarn (Thai)

Simons (Hebrew)

Not pictured:
Hungarian, Polish, Mandarin.

ALSO BY SARINA BOWEN & ELLE KENNEDY

TOP SECRET by Sarina Bowen & Elle Kennedy

GOOD BOY by Sarina Bowen & Elle Kennedy

STAY by Sarina Bowen & Elle Kennedy

HIM by Sarina Bowen & Elle Kennedy

US by Sarina Bowen & Elle Kennedy

Made in United States
North Haven, CT
16 August 2022

22808274R00043